THE LITTLE BEAR WHO SUCKED HIS THUMB

Written & Illustrated by
Dr Dragan G Antolos

Published by Dr Dragan G Antolos
292 Manningham Road, Lower Templestowe, 3107
Victoria, Australia
Email: dragan@oliverthebear.com

National Library of Australia
Cataloguing-In-Publication

Antolos, Dragan G., 1959-.
The Little Bear who Sucked his Thumb

3rd. ed.
For children
ISBN 9780980319804

1.   Thumb sucking—Juvenile fiction. I. Title

A823.4

Printed in China through Trojan Press

For my girls Ellen, Hayley & Lesley

In a green wooded forest far, far away, there lived a little bear called Oliver. Oliver was like other little bears his age. He loved ice cream, except strawberry, he loved cake and he loved to play chasey, but best of all Oliver loved to suck his thumb. It made him feel good. He would put that thumb in his mouth when he was tired during the day, even when he wasn't tired. Sometimes he felt like sucking his thumb, but before he even put it into his mouth, he would realize it was already there. This made him smile because it was like a pleasant surprise.

Most of his friends didn't suck their thumbs, and Oliver wondered if they knew what they were missing. Adults would often comment on how cute he looked, with his thumb and all. This made him go red and shy. Even though they meant well, it was a little bit annoying. But most annoying was Rochester.

Oliver did not like Rochester. He was a little bit older and would tease him about his thumb sucking. When Oliver got really mad he would go tell his Dad. "Don't take any notice Oliver", he would say. "When you are ready to stop sucking your thumb you will know."

The next day Oliver walked past Rochester and
removed his thumb just long enough to poke his tongue out.

That night, while his Mum was tucking him into bed, Oliver
asked, "Mum why don't adults suck their thumbs? His Mum
smiled. "Big bears don't suck their thumbs Oliver, only baby
bears. You will stop when you are ready."

Oliver thought about this as he put his thumb in his mouth. "Could you tell me the story about the dragon again?" Oliver loved those stories. Mum said they were only stories but Oliver thought they must be real. His Mother began, "In the deepest, darkest part of the forest, there lived a ferocious dragon ...." Oliver listened and quietly drifted off to sleep. ... suck ... suck ...suck...

The next day Oliver played in the forest like any other day. Mrs Panda rode by on her bike, and gave a wave. 'What a nice lady,' Oliver thought, smiling broadly.

"**M**ind you don't make those teeth crooked with all that thumb sucking, dear," Mrs Panda replied. Oliver's smile dropped down his face. "Bears look funny with crooked teeth you know," she added.

"How annoying." Oliver was a little cranky now. "*She* can't talk – a bear with big black spotty spots. I can stop sucking my thumb any time I like", Oliver told himself defiantly. "I am not a baby bear anymore."

He pulled out his thumb. POP! Oliver suddenly felt very pleased with himself. In fact he ran home excitedly to tell his mum and dad of his decision.

Oliver knew exactly where to find the dragon. The stories always began '.... in the deepest, darkest part of the forest..." so that is where he would go.

The next morning Oliver jumped out of bed, grabbed his lunch and headed straight into the forest. Oliver had travelled a long way. The forest became very dark and very quiet. He was feeling a little bit nervous. Maybe Mum was right, maybe there were no dragons.

Suddenly, he heard a noise ….suck…suck…suck. He spun around. There it was again ….suck…suck…suck. "Oh my goodness," sighed Oliver. He was sucking his thumb again. He pulled it out with a loud POP! That was kind of funny, he giggled. 'I must be getting a little hungry,' Oliver thought, and he sat down and unpacked his lunch.

'Yum, two chocolate cookies and two juicy apples.' His Mum always told him he had to have healthy food too. Oliver didn't mind. He quite liked apples as well as cookies. Oliver was just about to bite into his cookie, when he was knocked clean off his feet by the loudest, meanest roar he had ever heard. To make things worse, a giant flame swept past him, leaving the trees black and bare. Oliver jumped behind a rock to hide.

"RRRRRRROARRRR!!!" another loud, ferocious roar. Then there was silence.

Oliver was on the ground with his hands over his head and his eyes closed. He was sure he would be gobbled up.

"Oh, I'm so frightfully sorry," said an apologetic voice.

Oliver opened one eye, and came face to face with the biggest creature he had ever seen. Smoke was billowing out of its huge nostrils and two great wings folded into its body as it blinked curiously at Oliver.

"I hope you are not hurt lad. What are you doing in these dangerous woods – hey?" Oliver slowly stood up, and dusted himself off. *'What do you say to a dragon?'* he thought.

"ant a cookie?" Oliver replied.

The dragon looked surprised, then suddenly rose up on its powerful back legs and with its long neck extended above the trees, laughed out loud, occasionally releasing a ferocious burst of flame. Oliver could see tears rolling down its cheeks.

"Do...I...want...ha ha.... a cookie?" the dragon repeated, trying to catch his breath. "Me, a ferocious full-grown dragon nibbling a cookie!" He laughed out loud again. "By Jove, lad, dragons don't eat cookies!" He wiped the tears from his eyes, then leaned his head very close, as if to whisper a secret. "But I will have one of those apples if you don't mind."

Oliver sat with the dragon and chatted as they ate lunch. He told the dragon about his problem. He wanted to stop sucking his thumb but he just couldn't. He would always forget and it was especially hard when he was asleep. The dragon listened quietly.

"Well," he finally said, "I am more used to saving princesses and battling giants and trolls, but I can see that you have a problem."

The dragon slowly leaned forward, his huge head was so close that Oliver could feel his hot breath. Oliver felt a little nervous. The dragon could easily swallow him in one gulp. There was a long silence. Quietly the dragon asked, "Are you really, really ready to give up sucking your thumb?"

"I am not a baby bear any more, Dragon, and I am determined to do it." Oliver answered.

The dragon pulled back and seemed to smile. "I like your attitude young Oliver. Let's get to work then shall we?"

"It seems to me the problem is YOU want to stop but your thumb doesn't," chuckled the dragon. "However let us not forget that YOU are the boss and not that little wrinkled thumb of yours." Oliver frowned as he inspected it. "What do you mean wrinkled?"

The dragon completely ignored Oliver's protest and continued. "What that thumb of yours needs is a reminder."

"A reminder?" asked Oliver. "What do you mean?"

"Put this on your thumb Oliver," said the dragon producing a box full of what appeared to be colourful band-aids.
 "But I don't have a sore thumb." Oliver protested.
"You need a reminder Oliver. Now put one of these band-aids on your thumb." insisted the dragon.
Oliver shrugged his shoulders and wrapped the band-aid around his thumb.
"Good," said the dragon. "Now put that thumb in your mouth." Oliver looked puzzled. "But it has a band-aid on it."

"Exactly!" roared the dragon. "This, young Oliver, is your reminder. It will remind you when that little thumb of yours has snuck back in. The rest is up to you." The dragon handed Oliver the box of band-aids. "They're also good if you skin your knees," added the dragon.

"Now I must go Oliver." The dragon stretched his giant wings and was just about to leap into the air when he felt a tug on his tail. He looked down. It was Oliver.

"Dragon, when will I see you again?" The dragon smiled and looked down at Oliver affectionately.

"Take this my boy," said the dragon handing Oliver a small book and a pouch full of glittering gold stickers. Oliver flipped through the pages. He looked up at the dragon puzzled.

"But the book is empty."

"It is now Oliver, but every day that you remember not to suck your thumb I want you to put one sticker on the page. When you have a sticker on every page I promise to come back to see you."

With a powerful stroke of his wings
and a ferocious roar, the dragon
soared into the sky.
"Good luck lad," he called as he
disappeared into the clouds.

liver was very excited when he got home. He had already carefully placed a bandaid around his thumb and was feeling very proud of himself. He told his mum and dad about his adventure. He showed them his book, and his glittering gold stickers.

They thought it was a great idea and as the days went by they were very impressed with the number of stickers in the book. Oliver told them that when the last sticker was in the book the dragon would come to visit him.

"Oliver, dragons aren't real," his Mum said. No matter how hard he tried he could not convince his parents that the dragon was real.

Well at least Mrs Panda wasn't nagging him about his thumb sucking any more. And much to Oliver's surprise, even Rochester had stopped teasing.

The day finally came when Oliver put his last sticker in the book. He ran to tell his Mum and Dad.

"Mum, Dad, this is the day the dragon will come!"

"Oliver there are no dragons," laughed Dad.

"But he promised and I know he will come."

"That's a very good imagination you have Oliver," smiled Mum.

"Now off to your room and get ready for bed!"

"Yes Mum," Oliver sighed. 'I know it sounds strange, dragons and all, but I wish they would believe me.'

Oliver went to his room and looked out the window.
He could hardly believe his eyes.

"MUM, DAD COME LOOK!!......."

THE LITTLE BEAR WHO SUCKED HIS THUMB

For more information regarding thumb sucking, or to purchase additional books, personalized wall charts with stickers and gold pouch, visit
www.oliverthebear.com

www.oliverthebear.com

Other books available in the 'Little Bear' series, with Oliver and his friends:

LITTLE BEAR BEWARE

ABOUT THE AUTHOR

Dragan Antolos graduated as a dentist in
1982, and is married with two daughters.
He has a general dental practice in
Melbourne, Australia.

By Hayley